GIORGIO
SALATI

CHRISTIAN
CORNIA

The Gang of the Feline Sun

WHAT ARE YOU DOING?
I'M CHASING A CAT!
LOOK! HE WENT INTO THAT HOLE!
GRRR! I HATE CATS!
WAIT FOR ME!
PLOF
WE LANDED IN A THEATER! BUT WHAT MOVIE IS THIS?
SSSHH!
OH, NO! IT'S A MOVIE ABOUT CATS!

To Daisy, Susy and Tea: the flowers of my garden.

–*Giorgio*

To Erika for her continued support, to Tommy,
And to Otto, Leo, Samantha, and Nicole for their "hairy" company.

–*Christian*

Special thanks to Teresa Radice & Stefano Turconi, Marie Garot, the editorial team at Topolino, Ken Anderson, and Milt Kahl.

#1 "The Gang of the Feline Sun"

www.papercutz.com

GIORGIO SALATI — Script
CHRISTIAN CORNIA — Art, Color, and Cover
ERIKA TURBATI — Color Assistance
MASSIMILIANO CLEMENTE — Original Editor
ALESSANDRO AURELI — Lettering and Layout
OLIVIA ROSE DONI — Translation
Foreword by FRÉDÉRIC BRRÉMAUD and FEDERICO BERTOLUCCI
Special Thanks to CECILIA RANERI

JEFF WHITMAN — Editor, Production
IZZY BOYCE-BLANCHARD — Editorial Intern
JIM SALICRUP
Editor-in-Chief

Papercutz books may be purchased for business or promotional use.
For information on bulk purchases please contact
Macmillan Corporate and Premium Sales Department at
(800) 221-795 x5442.

Hardcover ISBN: 978-1-5458-0425-4
Paperback ISBN: 978-1-5458-0426-1

Printed in China
January 2020

Distributed by Macmillan
First Papercutz Printing

Warm sun and fresh air, with a hint of fir trees. Something totally new for Brina.
I'VE NEVER BEEN HERE BEFORE.
It's the mountains.
AAAHH!
FINALLY... VACATION.
AND FREEDOM.

SAM, I WANT TO SIT MYSELF DOWN AND DO NOTHING AT ALL.
I'VE BROUGHT THAT HUGE UMBERTO ECO BOOK I NEVER GOT DOWN TO READING.
GET OFF, BRINA. YOU'RE MESSING EVERYTHING UP.
COMING, MARGRET!
NOT YOU, BRINA. YOU HAVE TO STAY INSIDE.
MEOW
MEOW
MEOW
MEOWMEOW
MEOWMEOWMEOWMEOWMEOWMEOWMEOW
WHAT DO YOU THINK? SHOULD WE LET HER OUT?
MEOWMEOWMEOWMEOWME

I HOPE SHE DOESN'T RUN OFF.
WOW!
IT'S FULL OF PREY! NONE OF THESE IN THE CITY...
...IT LOOKS LIKE SHE'S CAUGHT SOMETHING.
WHERE IS SHE?
SHE'S DOWN THERE PLAYING, AND...

I READ THAT CATS BRING THEIR VICTIMS TO THEIR OWNERS AS A GIFT.
THANKS, BRINA! IS THAT FOR ME?
CRUNCH
CRUNCH
OH! IT WASN'T FOR ME.
UGH!
COME ON, RASCAL. IT'S TIME FOR SUPPER FOR HUMANS TOO!
That night, thousands of tiny, shining eyes are peering down from the clear mountain sky.

And the following morning, the scent of herbs and prey instills a new energy in Brina.

WHERE DID SHE GO?
I CAN'T SEE HER ANYMORE.
DO YOU THINK SHE'S RUN OFF?
BRINA!
WHO ARE YOU?
MY NAME IS VESPUCCI, AND I AM A FREE CAT.
BRINA?
MY OWNERS ARE CALLING ME.
YES, YOUR OWNERS. YOU ARE THEIR PROPERTY, THEN.

LISTEN TO ME: SHEEP HAVE OWNERS, NOT CATS.
BUT... THEY'RE MY FAMILY.

IF THEY WERE YOUR FAMILY, YOU'D WALK ON TWO PAWS AND WOULDN'T HAVE A TAIL. BUT YOU DO -- YOU'RE A CAT.
YOU'RE JUST A TOY FOR THEM, A CUDDLY TOY TO PLAY WITH. THAT'S WHY THEY KEEP YOU.
THEY USE YOU, BRINA.
NO. THAT'S NOT TRUE. THEY LOVE ME!

BRINA!
I NEED TO GO NOW.
SO THEY CAN LOCK YOU INDOORS?
THEY WILL ALWAYS BE FREE TO DO WHAT THEY WANT. YOU WON'T.
I...

BRINA? WHERE ARE YOU?
I'M GOING BACK.
REMEMBER...
...WE WERE BORN TO LIVE IN THE WILD, NOT TO BE USED AS PLAYTHINGS.
THERE SHE IS!
SILLY GIRL, WE WERE CONCERNED!
LET'S KEEP HER INSIDE, I WAS SO WORRIED...
OKAY...
THEY WILL ALWAYS BE FREE TO DO WHAT THEY WANT...
WE WERE BORN TO LIVE IN THE WILD.

In the mountains, life goes by slowly for people, but for cats it's constant challenges and adventure.

ARE YOU READY?
JUST A MINUTE, I'M COMING.

NO, BRINA, YOU'RE STAYING HERE.

How long can a young cat's thirst for adventure be denied?

ERMARK
ROBIN HOOD AND LITTLE JOHN WALKING THROUGH THE FOREST, OO-DE-LALLY, OO-DE-LALLY, GOLLY, WHAT A DAY!
MEEEEEEOOOOOOOWWWWWWWWWWWWW
POOR THING, SHE'S MISERABLE.
SHE REALLY WANTS TO COME OUT... I GUESS WE ALWAYS KNEW SHE WAS AN EXPLORER.
I HAVE AN IDEA!

WHERE DID IT GO?
HERE IT IS.
THE HARNESS?
YES, AND A LEASH AS WELL...
BE STILL, BRINA.
WE'LL TIE HER HERE, THAT WAY SHE CAN'T GO FAR.

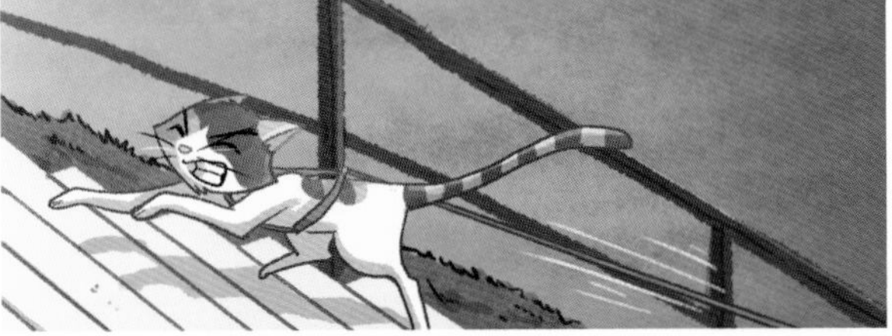

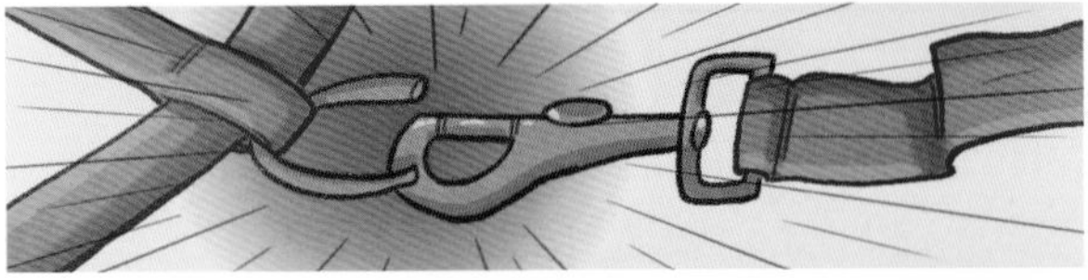

GRR...
WOOF

HUH, LOOK WHO'S BACK. DON'T TELL ME YOU FREED YOURSELF FROM YOUR PRISON?
EXACTLY.

YOU WERE RIGHT. I WAS BORN TO EXPLORE THE WORLD, AND NO HUMAN CAN STOP ME.
GOOD. I THINK YOU'RE READY TO BE A TRUE CAT.
YOU BET!
OKAY, I'LL TAKE A CHANCE ON YOU. FOLLOW ME.
03
BRINA, LET ME INTRODUCE YOU TO THE GANG OF THE FELINE SUN.
MY NAME IS GABRIELLE.
I'M ATOM.
YOU CAN BE PART OF THE GANG, IF YOU LIKE. AND TO SHOW YOU WHAT IT MEANS TO BE IN A CREW LIKE OURS...

...FIRST OF ALL, THE GANG WILL DO SOMETHING FOR YOU.
HEY, SMELLY DOG! SLOBBER BALL!
!
YOU CAN BARK ALL YOU LIKE, YOU DON'T HAVE ENOUGH PAWS TO CATCH ME.
WAF! WAF!
GOOD MORNING, GERALD.
?
ARF! ARF!
DONE! NOW THAT BIG BALL OF TICKS WON'T BOTHER US ANYMORE.
THANK YOU, FRIENDS. YOU WERE BRILLIANT!

HEY, LOOK AT THIS!
BRINA...
SHE RAN AWAY...
WHERE CAN SHE HAVE GONE?
MAYBE SHE WENT DOWN THERE AGAIN?
NO... SHE'S NOT HERE.
BRINA...
BRINA!

THE GANG OF THE FELINE SUN HAS AN OFFER FOR YOU, BRINA.
NOW, IF YOU REALLY WANT TO BE PART OF OUR CREW, YOU NEED TO WORK FOR IT.
ALRIGHT, WHAT SHOULD I DO?
LET'S GO OUT ON PATROL.
WE'LL DEFINITELY FIND SOMETHING FOR YOU TO DO.
BRIIINA!
MY... MY OWNERS ARE LOOKING FOR ME.
IF YOU GO BACK TO THEM, IT'S FOREVER.
LET'S GO.

LET'S ASK AROUND, MAYBE SOMEONE HAS SEEN HER.
YES...
YOU GO THAT WAY. IT'S BETTER TO SPLIT UP, ISN'T IT?
YES, I... I'M JUST AFRAID THAT--
DON'T WORRY, SHE MUST BE SOMEWHERE AROUND HERE.
I HOPE SO...
FIRST THING YOU HAVE TO DO IS GET TO KNOW THE PEOPLE WHO ROAM OUR TERRITORY.
THESE ARE THE STEINERS. HARMLESS AND SILLY. THEY ARE SLOW, SO THEY POSE NO DANGER TO US.
AND THIS IS THE WARNER FAMILY.

ALWAYS GETTING INTO TROUBLE.
STAY STILL FOR A SECOND.
THEY'RE THE OWNERS OF THAT AWFUL DOG.
THE GROWN-UPS ARE HARMLESS, BUT THEIR HORRIBLE CHILDREN MIGHT WANT TO ADOPT ONE OF US.
HUMANS... DISGUSTING!
AND THESE ARE THE MASOLETTIS.
HE IS HIS MOTHER'S PUPPET. SHE'S A REAL WITCH WHO NEVER LEAVES HOME.
PERHAPS THIS IS THE CHANCE FOR YOUR TEST.
YES!
LET'S PRANK THE MASOLETTIS! LET'S DO IT!
CALM DOWN, ATOM.

I NEED TO THINK ABOUT IT.
≡MMRROW!≡ TAKE THAT, YOU WITCH!
I HAVE AN IDEA.
NOW'S THE TIME, BRINA. IF YOU REALLY WANT TO BE PART OF THE GANG OF THE FELINE SUN, YOU'LL HAVE TO COMPLETE A MISSION.
IF SHE CAN'T, CAN I DO IT FOR YOU?
DON'T BE SILLY. SHE MUST DO IT.
YOU'RE RIGHT, VESPUCCI. SORRY, VESPUCCI.
SO, BRINA, ARE YOU READY FOR YOUR CHALLENGE? ARE YOU SCARED?
SCARED? ME?
I'VE WAITED ALL MY LIFE FOR THIS MOMENT.
ADVENTURE, AT LAST!

NO, I'M SORRY, I HAVEN'T SEEN ANY CATS.
ME NEITHER.
OKAY, THANKS ALL THE SAME...
GOOD MORNING, MR. AND MRS. STEINER.
EXCUSE ME?
I SAID "GOOD MORNING"...
AH, GOOD MORNING TO YOU TOO.
YOU DIDN'T HAPPEN TO SEE A WHITE CAT WITH GRAY AND LIGHT BROWN SPOTS?
A CAT...?

HAVE YOU SEEN A CAT?
EXCUSE ME?
A CAT.
YES, OF COURSE I HAVE.
YOU HAVE? YOU SAW HER?
YES, EVERY EVENING, BY THE SEA.
BY... THE SEA?
OH, YES, YOU SEE WE HAD THIS HOUSE, YOU KNOW, IN THE '70S— WE DIDN'T HAVE ANY GRANDCHILDREN AT THE TIME. ROB AND GRETA ARE OUR GRANDKIDS'S NAMES. SHE'S ELEVEN, NO... HE'S ELEVEN, AND SHE'S EIGHT...
ANYWAY, OUR GRANDKIDS USED TO PLAY WITH THIS BLACK CAT... OR WAS IT OUR KIDS?
IT'S OKAY... THANKS ANYWAY.
I REMEMBER THAT FAMILY OF CATS THAT USED TO LIVE IN THE WOODSHED.
THAT WAS WHEN YOU USED TO GO TO THE LAKE AS A CHILD, OTTO.

HELLO. HAVE YOU BY ANY CHANCE--
STAY STILL.
WHAT?
I WAS WONDERING IF YOU'D SEEN A WHITE CAT.
NO, NO CAT. I'M SORRY, BUT I'M BUSY TRYING TO GET THIS PAINT OFF THIS WALKING DISASTER.
HOW ON EARTH DID YOU DO THIS...?
THANKS ALL THE SAME...

I JUST HAVE TO FIGURE OUT HOW TO GET IN WITHOUT BEING SEEN.
IT WON'T BE SIMPLE. THE WITCH AND HER MINION DON'T LEAVE THEIR POSITIONS OFTEN.
YES?
HELLO, HAVE YOU SEEN A WHITE CAT? WITH GRAY AND LIGHT BROWN SPOTS?
SOMETHING HAS CAUGHT THEIR ATTENTION.
THE MINION HAS LEFT.
PETER?
IF I'D SEEN HER I'D REMEMBER. I'D LOVE A KITTEN.

WHO IS IT?
JUST A LADY, MOM. SHE WANTS TO KNOW IF WE'VE SEEN A CAT.
THE WITCH HAS GONE TOO.
THE COAST IS CLEAR!
I MUST...
I MUST MAKE IT. I HAVE TO SHOW THEM THAT I'M A WORTHY FELINE.
WHOEVER IS AT THE DOOR... THEY'RE DOING ME A REAL FAVOR.
WE HAVEN'T SEEN ANY CATS. WE MIND OUR OWN BUSINESS HERE.
OKAY, OKAY.

ISH SHOOO HOTCH.
SLAM
G-GOODBYE.
THE PIE! THE PIE! WHERE IS IT?
IT WAS YOU, YOU GREEDY BOY. YOU DISTRACTED ME WITH THAT WOMAN...
MOTHER, NO! I SWEAR IT WASN'T ME.
DELICIOUS!
MY OWNERS NEVER ALLOW ME TO EAT PIES.
AND THIS IS JUST THE BEGINNING.
That's right, Brina. Just the beginning.

Sam fears that if Brina reaches the main road, she could be hit by a car.
BRINA?

But she's always been afraid of cars, she would never go near them.

Unless her desire for adventure has become too strong.

8.07

I COULDN'T FIND HER AND IT'S GETTING LATE. MIGHT AS WELL START OVER TOMORROW.

I WENT TO THE MASOLETTIS'S... I FEEL LIKE THEY'RE NOT TELLING ME THE TRUTH.
WHY?

WHAT IF THEY TOOK HER?

HOLD HER STILL, SON.

LET'S PAINT HER BLACK, SO NOBODY WILL THINK WE TOOK HER.
MUAHAHAH!
MEOWWW!

YOU'RE JUST IMAGINING THINGS. OUR BRINA IS TOO SMART AND QUICK TO LET SOMEONE SHE DOESN'T KNOW NEAR HER.
I KNOW, I KNOW.

No, Sam, it's useless to stand watch like the guardian of the lighthouse. Your cat won't just appear in the grass like the light of a boat lost at sea.
WE'LL FIND HER. DON'T WORRY.

AS YOUR SUPREME LEADER...
...AND AFTER THE SUCCESSFUL INITIATION OF OUR BRINA HERE...
I DECLARE HER AN OFFICIAL MEMBER OF THE GANG OF THE FELINE SUN.
MAOOOWWW!
HAND HER THE CEREMONIAL CROWN.
IT IS A GREAT HONOR FOR ME.
AND NOW LET'S FREE HER OF THAT HARNESS. IT IS THE LAST SYMBOL OF HER ENSLAVEMENT TO THE HUMANS.
I... I CAN'T...
LET ME TRY.
SO BE IT. THE LONG ARM OF THE HUMANS WILL HAVE TO STAY ON YOU FOR A WHILE YET, UNTIL WE FIND A SOLUTION.

I JUST CAN'T SLEEP IN THE BEDROOM.
I CAN'T EITHER.
WE COULD SLEEP HERE.
YES! THAT WAY WE'LL BE CLOSE TO THE DOOR, IN CASE SHE COMES BACK.
LEAVE THE DOOR OPEN! WHAT IF SHE COMES BACK AND SEES THE DOOR SHUT?
SHE'LL MAKE SOME NOISE, DON'T YOU THINK?
OR SHE MIGHT LEAVE AGAIN!
BUT I'M SCARED OF LEAVING THE DOOR OPEN AT NIGHT.
WHO DO YOU THINK IS GOING TO COME IN UP HERE? WE'RE NOT IN THE CITY!
BUT...
OKAY, I GET IT.
WHAT ARE YOU DOING?
YOU'RE NOT THINKING OF SLEEPING OUT HERE, ARE YOU? IT'S TOO COLD!
I AM. IF BRINA COMES BACK, I'LL SEE HER.

The air is clear and crisp.
The stars are like drops in a teary sky.
It would be a perfect night, if the young couple's hearts weren't beating softly, like bare feet on the thin ice of hope.
It would be wonderful to wake up and find the cat rolled up on his lap...
...like before. A very recent past for humans, but so long ago for a feline.
For the moment, there is only a near silence, never absolute, for that is the sound of Nature. Every creature distinctly recognizable. Except one.

Except Brina.
A MOUSE!
I GUESS YOU HAVEN'T SEEN MANY, HOLED UP IN AN APARTMENT.
SQUEAK!
WHAT JOY! I HAVEN'T FELT LIKE THIS SINCE...
...SINCE I WAS IN THE COUNTRY. THEN... THEN I WAS FREE.
GOT IT!
MOM! IT GOT AWAY!
DON'T WORRY, BRINA, THE NEXT ONE WILL BE YOURS.

I MISS MY MOM SOMETIMES.
SAVE SOME OF THE PREY FOR KALIMA.
WHO IS KALIMA?
A FRIEND WHO LIVES DOWN IN THE VILLAGE.
HER OWNER GIVES HER EXPENSIVE CAT FOOD, BUT SHE LIKES FRESH GAME BETTER. WE BRING HER SOME AND SHE GIVES US HER FOOD.
HMM, BUT YOU SEEM LOST IN THOUGHT.
I WAS REMEMBERING WHEN I WAS A KITTEN.
I LIVED WITH MY MOTHER AND MY BROTHERS.

THERE WERE HUMANS TOO,
BUT THEY LET US LIVE FREE.
EVERY NIGHT WE USED TO GO
INTO THE FIELDS...
...AND EXPLORE, AND HUNT.
THAT'S WHEN I FELT LIKE A TRUE FELINE.
AND WE NEVER CAME HOME
EMPTY-HANDED.

The morning sun peers over the mountains
like a child from under his bed covers.

And the cat hasn't
come back.

EXT EDITOR - BRINA1.PDF
ILE EDIT VIEW INSERT FORMAT
BRINA
LOST
YEAR-OLD
YOU'RE MAKING A FLIER...?
SOMEBODY MAY HAVE ALREADY FOUND BRINA.
WE CAN PRINT IT AND PUT IT UP AROUND THE VILLAGE, AND IF ANYONE FINDS HER THEY CAN GIVE US A CALL.
THERE'S A COPY SHOP IN THE VILLAGE!
PERFECT. I'LL GET DRESSED.

AND HERE ARE THE RAMBLERS!
GOOD MORNING, KALIMA. WE BROUGHT THE PREY, AS PROMISED.
A NICE BIG MOUSE. DELIGHTFUL!
THE CAT FOOD IS IN THE USUAL PLACE, EAT TO YOUR HEART'S CONTENT!
WHO IS THE KITTY WITH THE HARNESS?
A NEW MEMBER OF THE GANG.
CITY LIFE HASN'T CHANGED HER WILD WAYS.
IF YOU SAY SO...
ARE YOU JEALOUS? MAYBE BECAUSE SHE'S A BIT LIKE YOU?
SHE'S NOT LIKE ME IN THE SLIGHTEST!

CERTAINLY NOT IN TERMS OF CHARACTER. SHE HAD THE COURAGE TO LEAVE HER HOME, NOT JUST TAKE OTHER CATS' PREY.
DON'T GET IN A HUFF, YOU GRUMPY OLD CAT.
OKAY, TEAM, WE'D BETTER GO BEFORE KALIMA'S OWNER TURNS UP.
JUST A LITTLE MORE... NOM NOM
COPY SHOP
HELLO, WE NEED TO PRINT THIS FLYER.
ALRIGHT.
OH, WHAT A LOVELY LITTLE CAT. JUST LIKE MY KALIMA.
DON'T WORRY. THEY RUN AWAY, BUT THEY ALWAYS COME BACK.
THEY KNOW WE NEED THEM. THEY REALLY DO.

Brina's mind
is like a clear
blue sky.
She and her friends challenge
each other to see who can climb
the fastest up the huge gnarly trees
that stand guard in the forest.
In the meantime, Sam and Margret
put up the fliers in the village.
They might have to pay a fine,
but they don't really care.

Their concern for Brina pushes them to act
quickly. Sam wants to get everything
finished as soon as possible.

While Margret's mind is fighting back her
emotions. Like a pond whose surface
is constantly disturbed.

The couple chases passersby.
They politely listen to stories that have nothing to do with their search and which they don't really want to waste time on.
YOU KNOW, UP UNTIL LAST MONTH WE HAD A LOVELY LITTLE BLACK CAT...
Meanwhile, Brina is busy chasing all kinds of prey.
Those who manage to escape her go tell their friends what happened to them.
A quick break, drinking from the stream like true wild animals.
And bingo! The first catch as a liberated cat. Time for a snack, finally.

Time for a snack for Sam too: his stomach is rumbling, aided by stress. Margret doesn't understand: how can he possibly eat right now?

Why spend money, when there are fountains and wild strawberries galore? Sam can't understand: how can she think about money right now?

"We shouldn't have let her out."
"She's a city cat, she's not used to being out."

Sam tries to console her: Brina might be a city cat, but she was born in the country. She has her wild instincts, she'll manage just fine.

Instinct.
Instinct tells Sam to check under the cars.

His heart skips a beat.
But it's not her. She just looks like her.
"It must be the cat of the lady from the copy shop," says Sam.
"This is what our Brina looks like," they say, pointing at the flyer. "We mustn't forget her.
BRINA
LOST
2-YEAR-OLD TABBY.
IF YOU FIND HER,
PLEASE CALL US
AT THIS NUMBER:
555-555-3706
"Ever."

BRINA
LOST
2-YEAR-OLD TABBY.
IF YOU FIND HER,
PLEASE CALL US
AT THIS NUMB
555-555-3706
I'VE SEEN FLIERS LIKE THESE COUNTLESS TIMES IN THE CITY.
YET, I NEVER REALLY PAID ANY ATTENTION TO THEM.
WHO'D HAVE GUESSED WE'D BE IN THE SAME SITUATION?
YOU THINK IT WOULD NEVER HAPPEN TO YOU, BUT THEN--
BRINA? BRINA!
SHE'S NOT HERE EITHER.
≡OOF!≡ FINALLY THEY'RE GONE.
BRINA
LOST
2-YEAR-OLD TABBY

WHAT'S WRONG? DON'T TELL ME YOU MISS THEM.
I DON'T, BUT...
BRINA
IT'S JUST THAT I FEEL SORRY FOR THEM. THEY WON'T KNOW WHAT TO DO WITHOUT ME.
NONSENSE. MY PHILOSOPHY WITH HUMANS IS: NO MERCY.
WHY ARE YOU SO ANGRY AT HUMANS? I GUESS YOU MUST HAVE A STORY TO TELL.
AN EXPLORER OF THE FELINE MIND, ARE YOU? ALRIGHT, IF YOU REALLY WANT TO KNOW, I'LL TELL YOU.
I WAS BORN TEN YEARS AGO, MORE OR LESS.
I REMEMBER THE COLORFUL DECORATIONS, THE WARMTH OF THE FIRE, AND A BOY. HE LOVED ME, AND MY MOTHER AND BROTHERS.

BUT A HUMAN CLAW RIPPED ME AWAY.
"FOUR CATS ARE TOO MANY," SAID THE OLD MAN. "WE HAVE TO GET RID OF ONE AT LEAST."
I FOUGHT WITH ALL MY STRENGTH.
I OWE IT ONLY TO MYSELF THAT I'M ALIVE.
HUMANS ARE SELFISH AND CRUEL. TRUST ME.

HELLO. I WAS WONDERING IF YOU'D PUT UP THIS FLIER...?
BRINA
LOST
HOW DO YOU HAVE IT ALREADY?
BRINA
LOST
SOMEONE IN THE VILLAGE TOOK A PICTURE AND POSTED IT ON FACEBOOK, SO I THOUGHT I WOULD PRINT IT OUT.
ARE YOU THE OWNERS? WE'LL FIND HER, YOU'LL SEE. EVERY SHOP IN THE VALLEY WILL HAVE THIS BY NOW.
THANK YOU...
THEY SEEMED SO COLD AND DISTANT, BUT REALLY...
THEY HAVE A GREAT HEART.

I'M HUNGRY.
I BET YOU HAVE A PLAN IN THAT HEAD OF YOURS.
YOU REALLY KNOW ME, GAB.
DO YOU REMEMBER THE SUNSHINE HOTEL?
It has a well-stocked kitchen and pantry.
LADIES AND GENTLEMEN, THIS IS BRANDO, CAT OF THE SUNSHINE HOTEL...
HI THERE, VESPUCCI. HOW ARE THINGS?
WE'RE JUST HERE FOR SOMETHING TO EAT, THEN WE'LL BE OFF.
OH, NO, GUYS, PLEASE...
HOLD HIM STILL.
DON'T DO THIS, VESPUCCI. YOU KNOW THE COOK WILL PUNISH ME FOR THIS...

GUYS, PLEASE... WHERE IS YOUR FELINE SOLIDARITY?
SHUT UP, BRANDO.
LET'S GO.
THIEVES... YOU'RE THIEVES AND LOOTERS.
≶AAAAAAH!≷ NOW I FEEL GOOD.
I BET! YOU ATE ALMOST EVERYTHING.
IT'S BECAUSE HE'S THE BOSS, STUPID.
What's happening, Brina? The taste of freedom isn't so sweet after all?
YOU EAT. I'M NOT HUNGRY ANYMORE.

I'M STARVING.
I CAN'T MAKE MYSELF EAT. I'LL JUST HAVE AN APPLE.
H-HELLO? Y-YES, WE'RE THE PEOPLE FROM THE FLIER.
I THINK I JUST SAW A CAT LIKE YOURS.
THANK YOU. YOU'VE BEEN SO KIND.
WHERE?
BEHIND THE SUNSHINE HOTEL.
LET'S GO!

PLEASE...
LET IT BE HER!
PLEASE...
LET IT BE HER!
THAT DARN CAT!
MEOWWW!
DISGUSTING THIEF!
IF YOU LIKE MY SEA BASS SO MUCH THEN YOU CAN FORGET ABOUT YOUR CAT FOOD!
ANOTHER FALSE ALARM...
IT'S NOT HER.
NO MATTER, WE'LL KEEP SEARCHING.
WE'VE LOOKED EVERYWHERE... LET'S TRY THE WOODS.

MY FRIENDS, IT'S BEEN A LONG TIME SINCE WE TRAINED IN ANTI-HUMAN SELF-DEFENSE.
LET'S GO TO OUR TATAMI ROOM.
REMEMBER: HUMANS ARE RUTHLESS BEASTS AND WE MUST BE READY TO DEFEND OURSELVES WITH EVERY MEANS.
I SURRENDER.
HA HA!

I WON.
WHAT ARE YOU DOING? WE'RE JUST TRAINING.
YOU WEREN'T READY.
VESPUCCI SAYS WE NEED TO BE READY AT ALL TIMES.
GABRIELLE IS RIGHT. YOU NEED TO FOCUS MORE, BRINA.
START AGAIN.
BANZAAAA--

...AAI!
BRINA IS RIGHT.
NOW YOU'LL HAVE TO FIGHT ME, LITTLE ONE.
HEY, TWO AGAINST ONE ISN'T FAIR.
YOU WEREN'T READY!
ATOM CAN'T POSSIBLY WIN. VESPUCCI IS TOO BIG FOR HIM.
YOU'RE... HURTING ME...
I THINK THAT'S ENOUGH, VESPUCCI. YOU'VE WON.

HELP! HELP ME!
LET'S GET HIM OUT!
WAIT.
HE HAS TO MAKE IT ON HIS OWN. I SURVIVED THE RIVER WHEN I WAS EVEN YOUNGER THAN HIM. ATOM HAS TO PROVE HE CAN EARN HIS FREEDOM.
AND IF THAT LEAVES JUST THE THREE OF US, THAT'S OKAY. A FEW DAYS AGO WE WERE A TRIO ANYWAY.
I CAN'T BELIEVE MY EARS.

TH-THANK YOU.
YOU... YOU WANTED TO KILL ME.
WHAT DOESN'T KILL YOU MAKES YOU STRONGER, EH?
I DON'T WANT TO STAY WITH YOU. I'M GOING BACK TO MY OWNERS!
SMALL LOSS, HE WAS JUST A WASTE OF TIME. I KNEW HE WAS WEAK.
YOU'RE A MONSTER. HOW COULD YOU DO THIS?

IT'S THE LAW OF THE JUNGLE, BRINA. YOU BEHAVED LIKE A HUMAN WITH ATOM.
YOU'RE CLEARLY STILL TRAPPED IN THEIR HYPOCRITICAL WAY OF THINKING. WILL YOU EVER BE FREE?
"THE LAW OF THE JUNGLE." YOU FOOL. WE'RE DOMESTIC CATS IN A MOUNTAIN FOREST, NOT BENGAL TIGERS.
I DON'T KNOW IF I BEHAVED LIKE A HUMAN, BUT I'M SURE I BEHAVED LIKE A FRIEND.
BUT MAYBE YOU'LL NEVER UNDERSTAND THAT.
THIS GANG IS JUST FOR YOU, SO THAT YOU CAN BE IN COMMAND. BUT I WON'T HAVE THAT, BECAUSE I'M TRULY FREE.
...AND I'M LEAVING.
BE MY GUEST, YOU WON'T LAST FIVE MINUTES WITHOUT ME.
MAYBE... BUT NOT WITH YOU, EITHER.

AND YOU, GABRIELLE? DO YOU WANT TO FOLLOW THIS INDIVIDUAL, LIKE A DOG?
YOU BETTER GO.
I SEE.
IT'S FINALLY CLEAR WHO'S FREE AND WHO'S THE MASTER IN THIS "GANG."
CATS... HUMANS... I'M DONE WITH THEM. FROM NOW ON, I'LL BE ON MY OWN.
ON MY OWN!

DID YOU FEEL THAT? THAT DROP?
NO...
I THINK IT'S GOING TO START RAINING SOON.
THAT'S THE LAST THING WE NEED.
BRINA?
WAIT... IS THAT...?
NO, MARGE, IT'S JUST A ROCK.
WE WANT TO FIND HER SO DESPERATELY THAT--
WAIT A MINUTE... THAT'S NOT A ROCK.

BRINA...

IS... IS IT HER?

IT'S JUST...
A PLASTIC BAG.

BRINA!
BRINA?

Brina doesn't know who or what to believe.

Trust humans again? How could she,
if she can't even trust her fellow cats?

Brina is hungry, and cold,
and alone. But going back home
would be a defeat. Wouldn't it?

Brina's mind is no longer a clear blue sky.
The stars are hiding.
The only lights that shine in her
memories are her mother's eyes.

Brina was just a little over two months old when
Sam and Margret turned up at the farm.

HERE ARE THE KITTENS.
WE ALREADY HAVE THREE CATS
AND THE COWS TOO, SO WE
HAVE TO GIVE THEM AWAY.

CHOOSE THE ONE YOU PREFER. ALL OF THEM, IF YOU LIKE.
WE CAN'T TAKE MORE THAN ONE. WE LIVE IN AN APARTMENT, IN THE CITY.

THE ONE WITH THE COLORED SPOTS, THE FADED ONE...
IT'S A GIRL, RIGHT?
YES, IT'S A GIRL.

WHAT IS SHE DOING? SHE'S LICKING THE WALL?!

SHE'S SO FUNNY.

COME HERE, LITTLE FADED ONE.

SHE'S A REAL EXPLORER.

LISTEN, SAM. SHE'S PURRING.

HOW SWEET, SO SWEET.
AM I WRONG OR IS IT LOVE AT FIRST SIGHT?

WITH THESE FADED SPOTS, SHE LOOKS LIKE SHE'S COVERED IN DEW.
I KNOW WHAT WE CAN CALL HER: BRINA!

WE'VE MADE OUR CHOICE: BRINA.
ARE YOU TAKING HER NOW? WILL I WRAP HER UP FOR YOU? HEE-HEE.
WE BROUGHT A CARRIER.

MEOOOOWWW
COME ON... WE'RE WET AND TIRED.
YOU'RE RIGHT, AND IT'S GOING TO BE DARK SOON. WE BETTER GO BACK HOME.
MAYBE THE RAIN WILL CONVINCE HER TO COME BACK ON HER OWN.
DID YOU HEAR THAT?
NO...

Rain.
Cold.
It's best to find some temporary shelter.
But be careful not to turn it into something...
...permanent.

In the meantime, Sam can't stop thinking.
Brina has always been afraid of thunder. Why won't she come back?
She's out there somewhere and she's not used to this. Is she scared? Will she get sick?
DO YOU THINK SHE KNOWS HOW MUCH WE LOVE HER?
I'M SCARED SOMETHING HAS HAPPENED TO HER.

I... I'M TIRED OF CRYING. I NEED TO THINK ABOUT SOMETHING ELSE, AT LEAST FOR AN HOUR OR SO.
DO YOU WANT TO WATCH A MOVIE?
ALRIGHT.
YOU KNOW TYPHUS?
YES, MOTHER.
YOU KNOW WHAT IT CAN DO TO YOU?
YOU ARE NOT SAFE.

A glass splinter. What does it remind you of?
Margret and Sam.
STOP IT, STOP!
IVE NEVER SEEN SUCH A NAUGHTY CAT.
What were they worried about, do you think?

About the bowl they'd bought on their first vacation together?
About the expensive curtains, just recently hung up?
No, Brina.
DID SHE GET HURT?
IT DOESN'T LOOK LIKE IT.
They were worried about you.
BE GOOD, SILLY CAT.
VESPUCCI WAS WRONG. THIS HARNESS IS NOT A SYMBOL OF SLAVERY...
...BUT OF PROTECTION.
MARGRET AND SAM ARE NOT MY OWNERS...THEY'RE MY FAMILY. I HAVE TO GET BACK TO MY FAMILY.
AT LEAST, I HAVE TO TRY.

Hurt and exhausted...
...on a starless night...
...trudging through the mud.
Who would be able to find their way?
A real feline would.
Real felines have senses and instincts to guide them.
A real feline is not afraid of the biggest challenge, the most exciting adventure: going home.
And despite their limitations, even human senses can prove to be more developed.

Developed enough to hear certain sounds.
The softest sound of someone we love...
...who's coming back home.
BRINA!
SHE'S BACK... SHE'S BACK...
MY LITTLE KITTEN...
No need to go on about the rest of the evening.
Margret and Sam were so happy they didn't care about their towels getting muddy.

The glass splinter is a trophy from this misadventure.
Her bowls have been kept full, waiting for her return.
The food has never tasted so good.
HOW FUNNY, THE HARNESS STAINED HER HAIR. IT LOOKS LIKE A TATTOO.
IT'S OKAY, IT WILL FADE IN TIME.
You're right, Sam. Nothing matters tonight Except for one thing:
Brina is back.

That night the sky is a slippery surface that the clouds slide across, revealing the pale moonlight.
The stars are shining again in Brina's eyes. Now she feels like a real cat.
She finally understands what whiskers are for.
The incredible sense of smell.
Those sharp eyes that can see in the dark.
That keen instinct.
It's all to get back to those we love.

Time to clean, tidy, and pack.
Time for the two humans and the cat to go back to the city.
SO... YOU LET THEM PUT YOU IN EVER SMALLER CAGES.
A REAL FELINE, INDEED.

THERE ARE NO CAGES SMALLER THAN THE ONES WE MAKE INSIDE OURSELVES, MY FRIEND.
YOU WERE DISAPPOINTED BY HUMANS. BUT NOT EVERYONE IS.
YOU MIGHT BE WILD, BUT THAT DOESN'T MEAN YOU'RE REAL FELINES. BECAUSE A REAL FELINE KNOWS WHO REAL FRIENDS ARE, WHETHER HUMANS OR CATS.
YOU WERE ABANDONED, AND THAT'S WHY YOU'RE JEALOUS. YOU CAN'T STAND THAT OTHER CATS HAVE WHAT YOU NEVER HAD: THE LOVE OF HUMANS.
MAYBE WE'RE NOT THE PROBLEM, VESPUCCI. MAYBE YOU ARE...
...AND YOU SIMPLY HAVE TO FIND THE RIGHT HUMAN.

LOOK, MARGRET.
WHAT IS IT?
I CAN'T BE SURE OF IT, BUT I THINK BRINA WAS MAKING FRIENDS WITH OTHER CATS.

OKAY, EVERYTHING IS READY.
LET'S SAY GOODBYE TO THE HOUSE.
LET'S SAY GOODBYE TO OUR FRIENDS.

IF THAT BEAST OF A COOK WON'T FEED YOU, THEN I WILL.

SHOP

WHAT IS IT, ATOM? WHAT CAN BE SO IMPORTANT?
AND FINALLY, LET'S SAY GOODBYE TO THE MOUNTAINS.

And the mountain says goodbye to you, Brina, a real cat who found freedom on her way home.

And after the mountain, it is the turn of the forest, the stream, the clouds, and the sun to all say goodbye.

A sun that looks over the peaks. A star that warms your steps, wherever they may take you. A new star that bounces inside you like the beat of a rattle, and makes you dance with its crystalline notes.

A free and welcoming sun.

A feline sun.

END

WATCH OUT FOR PAPERCUTZ

Welcome to the fast and furry-ious, first BRINA THE CAT graphic novel, by Giorgio Salati, writer, and Christian Cornia, artist, from Papercutz, those fuzzy-wuzzy folks dedicated to publishing great graphic novels for all ages. I'm Jim Salicrup, the Editor-in-Chief and Chief Kitten Wrangler here to talk about cats. Seems that there are so many cats featured in our graphic novels, that it's often suggested that we change our name to Paper*catz*. Obviously we must love cats, with BRINA THE CAT being just the newest addition to our feline line-up. Here's a list of some of the other cats you'll find at Papercutz…

Azrael – This naughty kitty belongs to the Smurfs's arch foe, Gargamel. Azrael would love nothing better than to eat a Smurf! You can find Azrael in THE SMURFS graphic novels by Peyo (writer/artist).

Azrael

Cartoon – Is a pretty happy cat, and he lives with Chloe and her family. CHLOE, by Greg Tessier (writer) and Amandine (artist) is published by Charmz, an Papercutz imprint focused on young love. Even though Cartoon is a minor character in CHLOE, he's proven so popular that he'll soon have a graphic novel of his very own.

Cliff – Is the pet cat of the Loud family and is just one of the many occupants of THE LOUD HOUSE. There's Lincoln Loud, his ten sisters (Lori, Leni, Luna, Luan, Lynn, Lucy, Lisa, Lola, Lana, and Lily), his parents (Rita and Lynn Sr.), and the other pets, Charles (a dog), El Diablo (a snake), Hops (a frog), Walt (a bird), and Geo (a hamster). Cliff may not be the star of THE LOUD HOUSE, but the fact is that the Nickelodeon animated series is a big hit, as are the Papercutz graphic novels, so who's to say he's not a part of what's making THE LOUD HOUSE so successful?

Hubble – Is the snarky pet cat of the Monroe family, and the unofficial mascot of the GEEKY F@B 5. Hubble has watched sisters Lucy and Marina Monroe, start up the Geeky F@b 5 with their friends, Zara, A.J., and Sofia, and tackle all sorts of problems, including finding homes for pets when the local animal shelter suffers major damage from a tornado. Even Hubble has to admit that when girls stick together, anything is possible!

Pussycat – Before Peyo created THE SMURFS he wrote and drew the adventures of PUSSYCAT. Pussycat is a lovable, mischievous tuxedo cat who spends his time chasing after milk and snacks and framing other members of his family for his shenanigans. This cat isn't exactly the noble hunting type; he'd rather play a game of kickball with the resident mouse than chase after him. Warning, our hero Pussycat is a real cat. He does not speak (he just meows) and his main passions in life are eating, hunting mice, avoiding dogs and meowing at night. All of Pussycat's adventures were collected in one deluxe volume entitled, PUSSYCAT.

Pussycat

Scarlett – Scarlett, as revealed in SCARLETT "Star on the Run" by Jon Buller (author/artist) and Susan Schade (author/artist), is a small, harlequin-colored cat and a huge movie star. And what's more she talks! Unfortunately she's also abused by her producer, so she dreams of only one thing: escaping! When the occasion presents itself, she runs for her life.

Sushi

Sushi – In CAT AND CAT by Christophe Cazenove (co-writer), Herve Richez (co-writer), and Yrgane Ramon (artist), when Sushi is adopted by Cat (short for Catherine) and her dad, their quiet life of living alone is over. Between turning everything into either a personal scratching post or litter box, and the constant cat and mouse game of "love me/leave me alone," Sushi convinces Cat and her dad that they have a lot to learn about cats.

Sybil – Is the cute cat owned by fourteen-year-old (soon to be fifteen) Amy Von Brandt. Amy's life is never dull, and you can find out all about her and Sybil in AMY'S DIARY by Véronique Grisseaux (writer) and Laëtitia Ayné(artist), based on the novels by India Desjardins, and published by Charmz.

We could go on and on, but we think you get the point! (We didn't even mention Geronimo Stilton's purr-sistant foes, the Pirate Cats, who in the GERONIMO STILTON graphic novels, are always trying to rewrite history to their advantage!) Instead, we'll just ask you to keep an eye out for the next BRINA THE CAT graphic novel, and to watch out for Papercutz!

Thanks,

JIM

STAY IN TOUCH!

EMAIL: salicrup@papercutz.com
WEB: papercutz.com
TWITTER: @papercutzgn
INSTAGRAM: @papercutzgn
FACEBOOK: PAPERCUTZGRAPHICNOVELS
FAN MAIL: Papercutz, 160 Broadway, Suite 700, East Wing, New York, NY 10038

Brina's Tale

She's a big-city cat
With a window-pressed face,
Looking at the world
In a car that races,
Whizzing through the trees
As she heads to the hills,
Owners up front, she's
Calm and chill.

Margret and Sam
Once adopted that cat:
She lived with her mom
On a farm before that...
She can't remember much:
It's a flash and a blur
'Cause she was still tiny—
A little ball of fur!

The vacation's begun!
They love the fresh air:
A big book in the sun—
They haven't got a care!
But I spoke too soon:
I hear a loud meow!
It's Brina's ringing tune:
She wants out...NOW!

To let her out's scary.
Will she find her way back?
Brina's not wary—
She'll explore the outback!

She takes a few steps;
She finds some new friends...
The local Gang of Cats—
They're just around the bend:
A bunch of cranky strays
Who hunt and live like beasts:
"Be free, like us," they say,
"The forest's full of feasts!"

She really likes her humans—
Dearest Margret, friendly Sam—
But woods are fun to run in:
She heads out, on the lam!
She leaps, she hunts, she fishes,
Playing tricks with old cans!
There's water when she wishes
She steals cakes from hot pans!
Filled with jubilation
She's feline fancy-free;
She's joined the jungle nation:
"No more litter box for me!"

At home, the house is sad,
They miss their cat that fled.
They walk and put up ads
And hope she's getting fed.
They search throughout the woods,
Looking up and down.
Is Brina gone for good?
No one's seen her 'round town!

Living wild seems fun
With her furry new friends,
But there really is a ton
Of strife without an end.
With fights and selfish acts
Life's NOT a piece of cake;
The gang's a cage, in fact:
It feels just like a fake.

The gang's no good for her!
She leaves: she knows her mind...
They're spiteful! They tease her!
She'll leave them all behind.
She leaps into a tree
'Midst heavy winds and rain.
She yowls where none can see.
She meows her lonely pain.

Sam and Margret miss her;
They're thinking of their cat!
Brina's thoughts are all a-blur:
Her heart goes pitter-pat
'Bout the house she used to live in
Where a kitten once she was—
Owners in the kitchen
Filled with happy, warm buzz!
Now she knows a home
Is family, not a cage!
They miss her: Time to roam
Back where there's no rage.

The night is dark and wet—
Wild winds, the forest dim.
Is this the way? Did she forget?
She risks her life and limb!
A cat can use her eyes,
Her whiskers, and her nose.
Her heart knows! Now she flies
As homeward bound she goes!

Sam and Margret wake—
Their hope is not yet dead.
A meow? Their hearts still ache;
They hope she hasn't fled.
And so it comes to pass:
They open up their door;
The cat they missed, at last
Stands soaking: hugs galore!

She's wounded just a bit;
Her fur is caked with dirt.
Blankets, tears, delight:
They're glad she's not too hurt!

Now the time has come...
Back to city lights.
Farewell to country cats—
Her eyes are shining bright.
Her friends they only were
A day or two or three.
Next year again they'll see her
For vacation, here she'll be.
Goodbye to mountains high,
To fir and scented pine,
To sun and air so delicate,
To joy without a whine.

They all go back together,
Sam, Margret, and their cat.
They know what really counts in life
Is love—and that's that.

Original text by Giorgio Salati
Translation and adaptation by Nanette McGuinness
Illustration by Cristina Giorgilli

?
WHERE ARE YOU GOING?
I HEARD A NOISE, MA. LIKE SOMEONE IS SCRATCHING AT THE DOOR...
WHO'S--?
OH, GREAT AND NOBLE FELINES! MAY OUR HUMBLE ABODE BE YOUR PALACE. MEOW AND I WILL SERVE YOUR EVERY DESIRE.
TO BE HONEST, GABRIELLE... THIS HUMAN DOES NOT SEEM ALL THAT BAD TO ME...